Beneath The Silhouetted Rainbow

Marcel Townsel

To My Dea[r] Ms. Sweetheart, Sheila Baldwin,

I thank you for all of your labors in pushing me to this reality!

The fact that you're holding this book in your hand is an example of something great that you've done — YOU KEPT ME WRITING, EVEN THROUGH THE PAIN, THE HURT AND ALL I DID NOT UNDERSTAND! THE THINGS YOU'VE DONE FOR ME ARE TO MUCH FOR THIS PAGE TO HOLD! THEY ARE FOREVER IN MY HEART. When I think of Upper Academia & Columbia, I'll always think of you. May you enjoy all your eyes Behold & May this be for you a great reading experience God Bless You!

Sincerely, Marcel Townsel

Sept 07 2001

Beneath The Silhouetted Rainbow
Copyright © 1997
Marcel Townsel

ISBN: 0-9710580-0-8
Library of Congress Control Number: 2001117492

First printing   August 2001

Additional copies of this book are available by mail.
Send $11.95 plus $2.50 for shipping and postage to:
BTSR @ Townsel Communications Co.
P.O. Box 0542
Chicago, Illinois 60690-0542
(773) 430-0568

Printed in the United States by:
Morris Publishing
3212 East Highway 30
Kearney, NE 68847
1-800-650-7888

Table of Contents

Preface 1

The Stories

Streetales of Lust 5
Streetales of Lust II 10
Beats 12
Making of The Middle Passage 13
The Busride 15
Metaphor II: Where Have I Been That I Can Help You? 18
B.L.U.E.S 21

The Poetic Soul

Introduction 25
Brown Sugar Don't Melt 26
Black Woman: Revolution 27
Magnolia 28
Wishful Thinking 29
Busy From The Mind–A Scolding 30
Romantica: Eden II (The Genesis of 7's Park) 32
Everywhere Was Eden 33
Nell 34
The Sea Too Is Africa 35
Oh Ole Preacha Man 36
Sho Nuff Wooped 37
My Beloved 38
A.J. II 39

The Meaning of Eulogy Square

Introduction 43
On Holy Rollers 44
Wednesdays 45
Dessert: A Eulogy 47

My Uncle Funny 48
Brown Bard Of The Baptist Church 49

The Silhouettes Of Soul

Natural High–1990 53
The Secrets I Kept 54
Black Romanticism 55
Feel–So–Sorry Syndrome 56
Love In Her Queensize Bed 57
The Open Letter: A Talking Drum Speaks 58
The Summer Sonnet of 1991 60
C–Note: She Moves Me 61

Acknowledgements 62
About the Author 63

Preface

A nameless character, whose pen gives you a glimpse into the various accounts of his youth, creatively, detailing some of his innermost thoughts and feelings, writes the following work of fiction. For the most part, he is an observer of the times, just as much as he actively participates. In many aspects, he's considered a pilgrim of life who analyzes it as he too, examines himself. As a man spotted with certain vices, he is also of a complex nature and at times, grieved with all he sees. Often, he is defined and typecast in many lights. Yet the important thing to this writer is that he defines himself by himself. For example, one of the many definitions of his existence can be found in the following lines:

"Beneath the silhouetted rainbow
I glow with melanin skin,
diggin the scene
the way my Daddy leaned,
as he held hid ground
on the west side of town,
during the year of '68,
as Madison Ave. burned down.
Beneath the silhouetted rainbow—
3rd World, multifaceted skin,
I hide, while smiling wide.
Yet there is an illusion to this mural—
centuries of pain that quake, bubbling over inside,
while I'm writing like Sir Arthur B., James,*
claiming the same—
that "nobody knows my name."
So I stand high, looking low,
as the volcano begins to erupt—
beneath the silhouetted rainbow."

*(James Baldwin, author 1924–1987)

In addition to the definition(s) of his existence, his reasons for telling **The Stories** of his youth are many. These accounts not only carry morals and stern warnings, but they are attempts to depict his realities

1

and the seriousness and severity of his own actions in society both, past and present. This is why he wrote *Streetales of Lust*. As a writer, he always wanted to know what really happened during the Middle Passage. The story, *Making of The Middle Passage*, is his brief version /interpretation of a bloody uprising aboard a ship bound for the Americas, which derived from several of his nightmares. In reading these tales, we find that the unidentified author possesses a great sense of spirituality from both, the past and the present. *Busride* takes you down a street in life that many have experienced, dealing with issues that our past will never let us forget. The nameless griot, as pilgrim and stranger, is on a quest, tirelessly searching for the meaning and metaphor of life. Writing for this unidentified individual is a celebration of love. It is also marked with the commemoration pain and various other experiences, expressed in *The Poetic Soul*: a short collection of passion filled lines. *Eulogy Square* pays a heartfelt tribute to the icons of one's childhood and the flood of memories that lounge between the lines. To the nameless character, these events are an ultimate culmination of the old adage the old folks told you when you didn't understand something or when they just wanted to wish you well. They said, "you keep on livin. Ya heaya. Just keep on livin." More than anything, they were speaking a blessing over your life. It's one of many phrases you rarely hear being spoken into the lives of today's youth. This one phrase gave you something...a tomorrow to look forward to. And when you got older...by and by...you understood exactly what they meant.

The Stories

Streetales Of Lust

Introduction

Lust is a very powerful force in society. It drives people to do the unmentionable and think the unthinkable. Someone once wrote, "experience is what you get when you didn't get what you wanted." This can often be the result of our lust. Here are a few examples of one of the most powerful forces known to man and how it affects society. This is not an attempt to glorify it, but to see it for what it truly is...

I.

What more can be said of Lust? For it is a montage / mirage that makes the world go round, or as reality would have it, "makes our heads spin around as we go around, out of minds in this world.

I spoke with a brother whose life was spent in the colors of green and red. A pimp he was and of high reputation. To his illegal harem he was known as "Sweet Daddy Fred." Sweet Daddy told me, "just as long as Lust kept me going, my whores would keep on whoring. Just as long as I have weak minds, oh, there will be a product. If some low-life gets capped in the process, hell, who cares?"

As the heydays of his nights rolled on, the whores kept on whoring, while a new generation of youngsters began gunning at one another. He finished our conversation by exclaiming, "out here, we do what we must. You don't think I'm caught up?"

II.

The next day, I went to the beauty shop to see what beauty there was in shop talk. Walking in, you know all eyes are going to be laid on you, whether you're fat, fine, skinny or scary-looking. Folks stare at you from head to toe, trying to figure you out–trying to undress you, (if you're a fine brother), pick your brains and see what you're all about.

And perhaps to some of them, If I didn't look like one of their baby's father, I could just be another brother trying to get some snatch. Now if I didn't pay attention to that one woman, you know the real pretty woman, I will surely be pronounced in her mind "GAY." On the other hand, when I walk into the shop, feeling unnecessary mean-spirited vibes and volatile tudes, I just might be the next prey upon which they'll vent their colorful, sisterly rage.

The young proprietor, who was a friend of mine said, "we normally don't do men's hair, but because we go back a ways, I'll hook you up with this phat style that I had a dream about. The beautician next to her tried to snap saying, "you're always dreaming! This aint the sixties. Nobody dreams anymore. These are the nineties and life aint nothin but a bunch of nightmares–nightmares of sadness and madness."

Slowly my friend turned around, wielding a hot comb in her hand, as if though she were about to fling it at the woman shouting, "I see dreams got you working in my shop. Now if you really and truly want a nightmare, keep on runnin off at the mouth." Suddenly, there was an unusual moment of dead silence that I've never heard in a beauty shop. Next, the flirtatious beautician ran up to me with a big kool-aid smile, asking, "hey sweet baby, what's your name?" Once I told her, she ran to everyone, pointing back at me and giggling with her associates. By the time she had finished, the monotony of silence was broken and everyone knew my name.

I thought to myself, "perhaps, it would do me no good to come up in here and not reap the fullness of the shop talk experience. So I stayed. Before I knew it, I was up under a shapely-sweet sistah's hands as she began to create a new look for me. Sistahs were talking about all sorts of "thangz"...about another sistah's man and how he hangs. One went on to comment as to how she'd put it on him, rocking his world and whipping him up like a batter of her old grandma's homemade pancake mix. As this conversation ended, a new one began. This time, it was hot and unimaginable.

One of the nail tech's clients came in to get her nails done, not out of necessity. She says it's just for fun. She brags, "girl, I do this stuff for all of my men. The last time you saw me, I had four, but girl, now I got ten! How I manage to handle it? I just don't know. I just take em as dey come and keep goin wif da flow. The tech said, "now how in the world do you think that you can manage this much?" She replied, "girl, my kids be needin things and I need some touch. I've got ten men; that's two per beeper. I know my stuff is going on. Girl, it's a keeper. My partner, the proprietor asked her, "well, what about HIV? Aren't you afraid?" She lashed back angrily, "I makes em all use a condom. I aint got no AIDS! Hell, I just can't help myself, but I gets what I want. I know my body is hot, coz I got lips hips..."

6

The more the conversation went on, she got louder and it got hotter. The nail tech rebuttled her, asking what if one of those men really cared. "Cares? Girl, I aint got time for carin. The wallet and credit cards are the only things that he'll be sharin wif me. Listen. let me tell you somethin and maybe you weren't raised this way. When it comes to men, I will use them, abuse them, chew them up, dog them out and lay em aside...in the gutter. There are no feelings cept between my legs and I will use it to squeeze him and every cent out of his pockets. Like I said, I know my body is good, coz I got just what they want;...the whole nine."

III.

After receiving my new hairdo, a disturbing news bulletin captured our attention. An eleven year old boy had killed another for his starter coat and gym shoes. His lust had brought about a fifty year prison sentence and another family's gut-wrenching grief. Leaving the beauty shop, I reflected on the news report. The suspect and his older brother conspired, together, to steal the victim's coat while all of the children were at recess on the school playground. From my past experiences of being a child, playing on school grounds, I see how this situation could have happened and also how it could have been averted.

The children were playing together when a fight broke out in the corner, by the fence, which separated the school from the alley. The children ran to see the fight and what the ruckus was all about. As the chaotic situation grew worse, the teachers took notice and rushed to quell the madness. By the time they headed toward the crowd, gunshots rang out. One kid's voice shrieked above the noise like an opera singer during a tragic scene, signaling that he'd been struck by a bullet. The curious rushed away from the boy. His starter jacket was then ripped from his bleeding body and tossed to a group of ruffians on the other side of the fence. As the teachers ran swiftly to the boy's aid, another ruckus was brewing.

The girls who were jumping double-dutch accosted the boy with the gun. The weapon was retrieved. Police, who were routinely patrolling the area picked up the boys in the alley. When taken into custody and questioned, the boy broke down in tears. He began explaining that the gun was given to him by his older brother and that he only meant to scare the boy–not kill him. The juveniles would be tried as adults.

IV.

Returning home from the shop, I reminisced on how list made two military buddies enemies. One wanted the other's wife. It costs him his stripes and both, he and his son's life. He wrote me a letter saying, "...we used to be pretty cool. One night, we were out at the club drinking, when he introduced me to his wife–an old acquaintance from high school. Suddenly, I remembered how bad I wanted her. To diffuse my feelings, I left their presence to mix and mingle in the crowd. Seeing her resurrected my buried crush and all the sweet poetry I used to write her. Back then, she was the epitome of beauty and there was no other. All four years in high school, my eyes only saw her. My ears were open to her every beck and call. My feet would run to her swiftly and religiously. The feverish infatuation that I had for her would warm me in the winter. I recount reaching for her in every way, but it was like chasing the wind. I wanted her in every dimension of my life imaginable. Oftentimes, I'd find myself projecting and directing my anguish over not having her onto positive avenues. I painted. I sang new songs. I danced. I wrote. No matter what I did, everything reflected my inner-longings for her.

Late that night, it was told to me that my partner's unit was going to the field. Returning to his table for a minor chat, I saw his disgust and felt his rage. His wife had just come to live with him for the duration of his tour. Now she'll be left alone, while he's out beating the bushes–unless he's on leave and didn't tell me. I know I shouldn't go after another man's wife, but before they were, it was us! The club was jumpin that night when the music suddenly stopped. It was officially announced that my partner's battalion had been placed on alert status.

People, left and right, were shuffling out onto the post and through the door which led to the outside of the main gate. My friend gave his keys to his wife and kissed her goodbye. He told her to call me for any assistance, in case of an emergency. After he left, she and I stayed at the club to catch up where we'd left off several years ago.

We agreed to go out on the town and talk. Knowing that it might not look right if we left out together, we left in fifteen minute intervals and met down the street on a dark corner. Finally, after five long years of dry tears and emptiness, two friends were reunited. We talked about us; how we used to feel, what changed those feelings and what we feel now.

Before we knew it, night had gone and daybreak was just an hour away. Leaving her that morning, I was determined not to depart as I had done in the past–unfulfilled. No, I yearned for fulfillment from my past. In order to quench the fiery flame within, I was determined to get it once and for all. Walking her home, to her door, I said my final words. She beheld the waterfall of want and streams of passion fill up in my eyes. Suddenly, she softly seized my head with two hands and planted her pleasure-sweet kiss on my lips. I felt myself sailing over her threshold. We collapsed on the couch and our clothes melted away from the fervent skin of our bodies. Our pores bursted open and the sensuous smell of sweat created a love-mist from which the rain of our souls flowed as we rolled.

In the heat of the love-mist, five knocks came to the door. I was my partner's special knock. We immediately got dressed and I hid in the closet. She sprayed her air deodorizer and opened the door. The sound of his voice sent tremors through my spine. I peeped to see her jump in his arms as her kissed her all the way to the bedroom. Creeping out of the closet, I rushed out the door and down the street. They ran out of the room to see what was going on. She began to panic hysterically. He gave comfort to her pseudo-weary mind, not expecting anything else. That morning, I reached post in just enough time to get ready for work. Later on in the day, she told me that she found my wallet in their closet and would have it returned anonymously. This was my first and last time doing such a thing; my own body and someone else's ring–a ring that once was gold is now rust, after the heat in the autumn rain and two lover's lust."

Your Friend,

Looking back on these three stories–these streetales of vicious vainglory; replicas and images of you and I, from the brother who committed lust once to the man with his "illegal wives," the people in this story could have been any one of us.

Streetales Of Lust II

V.

Growing up in church, I would often hear the preacher quote Galatians 6:7 saying, "Be not deceived; God is not mocked: for whatsoever a man soweth, that shall he also reap." As I recalled that memory, it sparked in me something that my old friend told me, as he continued sharing his breathtaking, lust filled experience, in his second and last letter dated 4-8-98.

He said, "Upon arriving to work, I found the schedule to be a bit different. I was to report upstairs to the first aid station to help administer the quarterly urinalysis test. One month later, the results came in with some earth-shattering news. I had tested positive HIV and to accompany my results were a set of orders and discharge papers. I'd be leaving in a week. Before I left, there was some unfinished business to settle. Inconspicuously, I notified my friend and her husband. We both confessed to our night of lust. He cried, but thought it not wise to lay a hand on me. In his words, I had been done in already. He and his wife rushed to the hospital for tests. Theirs came back negative. Leaving the hospital, the couple began discussing her actions and calmly making arrangements to divorce and send her home.

Nine months later, I received an anonymous letter in the mail. It was her writing. I opened the letter to find a picture of a newborn baby. The note said, "this is the result of our passion...our lust. Here is a small poem I feel from within that you once felt for me. Perhaps, it echoes the sentiments of our past experience;

"looking at (IT)–your body that is,
I (WAS) overtaken with the thoughts
of just how (BITTER) it wouldn't taste.
For the very air of your temple was (SWEET FRUIT) indeed!
Until I read between the lines, only to find out that...
(IT)
(WAS)
(BITTER)
(SWEET)
(FRUIT)...."

One month later, both, he and his baby died of AIDS. They had a closed casket ceremony. Then, they were cremated and their ashes were both combined and given to the winds over Africa. Before I went to bed, the nightly news caught my ears again, only to deliver more bad news. The pimp I spoke to the other day was found murdered in an execution style, along with the heavily materialistic woman I met in the beauty shop. The two brothers, who conspired against and killed the eleven year-old boy on the school playground, were both, shot and killed in a juvenile detention center riot. What goes around, comes around. That covers anyone of us who are overtaken, bound, driven and shaken by the evil known as LUST.

Beats

"At the gathering of the Elders, they played their drums skillfully. We heard them call as the rhythms drew us and we came to sit down at their feet to listen intently to everything they had to say. This is what we heard..."

–Marcel

Making Of The Middle Passage

It is said that the waters along the west coast of the continent are haunted and every year , during the season of heat, you can faintly see a mirage of untamed souls, giving testimony and bearing witness to how they resisted captivity, even if it meant sacrificing their own human lives. In the center of the crowd, there stood a Watusi warrior, whose eyes were a mysterious jet black. The windows to her soul had been shut, for she had taken her own life. Her attire told us that she was of royalty. Modern man, whose heart would palpitate when gazing at her glory, would say of her, "she's fine as the day is long."

Standing there that day, she began her testimony by saying, "my father is a chief tribesman. My mother–a weaver. This is my home, my land, my people. Why should I be taken away from it and them–against my own will? I recall vividly, the day we disembarked from shore how a rebellion broke out. They dropped our chains to feed us hot oats and to cool us down with salt water. Fiercely, at the sound of an ancient war cry, we charged our captors, seizing their muskets and whatever our eyes saw for weaponry. Their alarm sounded as the smell of blood and roaring canons filled the early morning air. The aroma of flesh and gunpowder sent messages to the sharks. As I fought with my brethren, I beheld the blazoning cannonballs mow some of us down; a head here and an arm there. The nerves sprang up from the necks of some, while their bodies went into shock, moving feverishly. The remains of fallen warriors were thrown overboard into the depths of the sea. We were not the only ones maimed and disfigured. There was a significant amount of them that were killed. The souls of our folk screamed out in a rebellion that said, "if we must die, let it be on our own terms, and if we must, live, let it too, be on our own terms." Hysterically, we rebelled as our bodies plunged to the sea, while theirs went to hell. The bludgeoning and mutiny continued until another slave ship pulled aside of ours.

Finally, we were outnumbered. Chasing me with shackles they did, until I successfully and deliberately robbed them of their satisfaction to rape me of my royal innocence. I ran until I leaped high into the air like a gazelle and plummeted into the misty cool waters. They will tell you that I jumped to an untimely death. Instead, I would have you to know that I only went to the ancestors prematurely. Everybody lost in the sea was not lost in the storm. The midnight waves that crashed against the sands delivered our edifices ashore. Some say it had turned out to be the saddest nights in our history. Once they both, the slave ships and the unslaved, shark-bitten bodies, started coming, they never stopped. Everyday, you could run to the Oceanside, expecting to see some loved one / kinsman washed ashore–disfigured and mutilated. Bloodstorms drenched, soiled and saturated our beaches. The sand was tanned, not by nature, but by the slaughtered, the slain–those mercilessly massacred, who felt that they had no place in a new world \ civilization.

Before the ravishing began, we were singing a song to the sun god. The great burning wheel rolled out of our sight as we sang saying, "Ma yen ndo yen ho. Ma yen ntena ase fefeefe. Mma yen mmfiri asaase yi so. Mma yen mmfa okwan bone so."*, meaning, "may we ever love this way, may we ever live this way, may we never leave this land, may we never go astray." Echoing these words, centuries later, I see women in old white cotton dresses, standing down by the riverside singing, "I shall not, I shall not be moved...." This was the place where they prayed to their God, asking for a sign that they had gotten themselves some of that "true, sho' nuff ole time ligion." As the troubled waters began to bubble over, they began doing their modern day Holyghost shout and dance. We sprouted up out of the water into their midst, doing the juba to the drumbeat of our ancient mother's heart. A divine communion had begun. There, in the Diaspora, a land familiar, yet unfamiliar to our souls, we dined with them as never before. Finally, it was time to depart. Leaving them in a whirlwind, our tears sang as they sucked us swiftly into the bubbling river. It was told to me that this river was the place where every African soul of the Diaspora was baptized. After this great movement, no soul that went into that water came out the same. No soul.

*(spoken in Akan)

14

The Busride

Last night, I left work only to endure a tumultuous trek home on the bus. Though tired from a long day, I felt no need to complain. I began to meditate quietly, thanking God for people that I've known, loved and heard of all my life. Considering where I sat, I whispered, "Lord, thank you for Rosa Parks." Even in my physically tired disposition, I know I could never be as tired as she was four decades ago, one December evening in rush hour traffic, trying to get home.

And in trying to reach her destination, the actions along the way would become one half the catalyst of our modern day struggles and movement toward social change. Those incidents and others that followed had come to try us in the fire once more. After all, it has always been my belief that the Middle Passage, the Great Enslavement, the Civil War and its aftermath tried us as silver in the oven. The Great Wars, African Colonization, Apartheid and the Modern Civil Rights Movement have tried us as gold. What shall be said of us tomorrow? Suddenly, my stop arrives as the question is answered inwardly, "Only God knows–only God."

On my way downtown this morning, I sat next to an African woman of the Diaspora. She was a bit stout, with a wide, mean face that spoke her worries, doubts and fears. Her head was wrapped in a blue scarf. Perhaps, if she'd show her glory, it wouldn't be so dreary in this place. If she smiled, instead of frowning, perhaps her face wouldn't look as if it was held hostage by some demon from Hell. As I took my place next to her, she moved over as if though there was more room. She turned her head to the scarred window and never looked around during the whole busride. She kept on moving and shifting as her body language resonated the ugliness of her soul. Her vibes said, "don't touch me and please don't say anything to me." Her face was affixed to the stained plastic window, engulfing the depressing views of the streets, as we passed through the various ethnic sections of town. Onward we rode, as her mannerisms began to say more than all that she had ever said aloud. She didn't want me to touch her. How can you not, accidentally, when the bus is carrying people beyond its designated capacity? She continued to speak in antisocial gestures saying, "don't touch me. The least thing I need is another man running lines on me." "Lines?" I am

15

young–young enough to be her son. By the way she looked that day...and she really wasn't a bad looking woman, I could just as well pass for her grandson. I glanced at her peripherally–not to judge her life, examine her soul and criticize her present state. I only wanted to compassionately communicate with her saying, "Mother–Sister, your pain, your grief I understand. I share it. I too bare it."

Looking at this woman here and there, with my peripheral vision, I began to look beyond the natural and see the spiritual. Beholding this woman in the spirit, I saw one downtrodden, deceived, despised and divided. Yet, she was not so downtrodden that she could not be uplifted. Neither was she so low in life that she did not get high. Most of all, I was never elevated beyond her that she relinquished the natural rights of being my elder. Knowing that she did not want to be bothered with the world physically, I began to talk to her mentally asking, "Mother, why do you treat me this way? Why don't you relax in your seat? What have I done wrong? I too, only want to sit down and catch my extra twenty minutes of sleep before I have to deal with the miseries of the day.

Do I remind you of a son, who displeased you so, that he lost himself to the evils of life and the wiles of the world? Tell me. Am I the son–the one spoiled rotten to the core, who had to have it all his way, which thereby deprived you of a golden opportunity? Heaven help if I favor his biological contributor, to whom you were promised to in matrimony, years ago. What happened? Did he run out, leaving you with a bastard child to raise, or did you catch him in bed with your sister and best friend? If so, what's your beef? I had nothing to do with that. I hope I don't favor the man you just fell out with, because he wouldn't pay your rent after you gave all to him last night.

Was it that you saw your best buddy–the weekend drinking partner, sucking face with your man in his wife's new Caddy? I don't have a beef with you. I'm not here to judge your life, especially when I'm standing in the need of prayer. The only thing I wish to say is that you don't have to move over to the point that you're plastered against the window. Believe me, I wash and bathe myself everyday, using plenty of deodorant. For you to move over as if though I were a leper, makes you no better a human than I. Look at us. We are both displaced, typecast and labeled....Society and statistics calls us "poor," but "poor" we are not! Economically disadvantaged sometimes, but we are never poor.

Listen to me lady. The clothes I wear and the one you wish for, makes us no better than one another. As you sit there, clutching your purse, you seem to forget how close we were, laying next to each other in iron-clad shackles, centuries ago.

Yes, we laid in various ships, shamelessly in each others filth, inhaling and exhaling one another's odor. We didn't care at the time. That wasn't even important. What was important? The fact that we knew ourselves and who we truly were. What mattered was getting through the voyage alive or getting off those awful ships, if we chose to do so. What matters most is never forgetting where we came from. We were our Mother, being raped brutally and severed from head to toe. Yes, in those days, we didn't seem to mind each other's plight, for it was our own. As for today, don't let me sit next to you, congested, in a sardine can car, carrying fifty people plus, voyaging through rush hour traffic and break wind or have hot, bad breath. Surely, you'd only call me out, cuss me out and cast me out. Have you stopped to think, all the way over there, that the very thing that you'd denounce was the same thing that you had no control over then, as you momentarily do not now?"

Finally, I arose from my seat, making my way through the maze of people. Instantaneously, I felt two huge eyes dart into my back–into my soul. She stared at me in disbelief, saying inwardly, "you have known my life. You have known my soul. I'm sorry brother. Please, forgive me, for had I known myself, I would have known you. I have treated you ill, and in doing so, I have disrespected myself. Truly, it was you, whom I laid next to and sailed with, only to be split up in divers places. Today, I do not love myself as I used to. I do not respect, care for and tend to the people as I did in those days. I hope you can forgive me. I didn't mean any harm." Getting off and looking back at the French-colored ferry, that floated upon asphalt carpets of the city, I finally caught a glimpse of her again. Through all of the people, she began to staring at me in the weirdest way, for she was a wanting soul, now wishing to communicate. Smiling benevolently, from within, I replied, "sister, I do."

Metaphor II :

Where Have I Been That Can Help You?

Last week, I left my professor's presence, on the brink of discovering the true meaning \ metaphor of life, according to my reality in this world. For it was echoing through the chambers of my Congo-beating heart.

It's like the rapid blood rush flowing through my veins.
Oft times flowing fickle,
at times flowing nice and slow.
Flowing,
Glowing,
Growing,
Going,
Flowing nice and slow.

Determined to find the metaphor, I made tracks back to the hood of my old stompin grounds to see the sights, to sense the smells and to hear those awful hungry sounds of pain. Nothing's ever like the black B.L.U.E.S.* rain of summer.

Sadly standing in stupidity, I see sweet, little, sassy soul sisters, simultaneously swearing back and forth, shouting about selling sweetness swifter than the rest.

Their cleavage is a showin,
their faces are a glowin
with crimson colored lips
and golden, sparklin fingertips–
wearin dem holey halter tops
and mini skirts, tight beyond da fittin–
3 inch satin color crimson heels
to match their sugardaddy's red hubcap wheels,
and those big, beerbelly bottle figured brothers, with Malt liquor
in their hands, boldly babbling and bellowing out blues tunes,
swoons and crooning crazy on the crowded K-town corner
of Keeler Avenue and Madison street,

while the church down the way rocks to a Sunday morning
sanctified, Holyghost shoutin beat. I smell the various vital
stinches pinching
my nose in such a way that you'd scream and shout, sneezing,
"hachoo, hachoo, hachoo!
I smell barbecue,
honeydew and Momma's roux.

It's Friday,
my day,
high day.
Some brother's spendin their pay
instead of tryin to make a way
for my boys and girls–
my world–
our world.

I see little boys getting slapped for tryin to shoot craps,
while a fatherless baby sits out on a partially-built porch
in his miserable momma's loving lap.
Her head is bowed down.
Her face features a foolish-hearted, fatal frown,
while Big Momma stands off to the side, hidden
in her rag tag evening gown,
lookin, listening to the ghastly, ghostly hell, ghetto sounds
of buxom browns screamin up and down the way,
as mutt hounds are grizzly crooning in the night.
Next door, two lovers are moaning and groaning
over feelings dat'll come to light in just nine months.
I know, becoz I've seen it all. I've heard it all and I sense it all.
This is my town too and I say that nothing's ever like the black
B.L.U.E.S.* rain of summer.

　　After leaving my old hood last night, I found myself returning in the
afternoon. Something brought me back. I got off at the somewhat
improved L stop with an open bay ramp that led to a newly improved
bridge and a somewhat half done road. On the corner, there stood an old
dingy red, weather beaten barbecue shack, with tattered pieces of
chipped off paint, slowly flying in the wind. The smell of the pork shack
would seize you in such a way, that if you had a few bones on ya, that

you were saving, it would burn a hole in your pants screaming, "take me there!"

The neighborhood liquor store sold everything that Lil Leroy could fathom in his mind For the store that sold the substance that he grew up on would also be the same store that sold the substance that he would die from. By the store, in the way, I saw broken bottles of red wine, malt liquor, and cheap beer, all aligned in the same gutter, standing, like all the men above them on Cool Folk's Corner; brokenhearted, idle, yet they were intermingled and integrated, but ran over–so much in so til the rolling wheels of life's circumstances pushed the very pieces of their lives to the four winds of the world and they, despairingly are broken apart, mixed up and thrown away.

Walking past Cool Folks Corner, in a swift motion is a pair of maternal twins, whose momma told them, "neva stop fa nothin, not even to give yo name. And boy, she'd say, you walk on the outside of the street corna, when you walkin wif yo sistah. Least thing I need now is a baby befo it's time. If ya wanna get high, get high on God tonight, in tarry service. Besta be sittin on the front row. And boy, keep yo ambitious, eva curious pants up, coz da so-called Heaven's minute you let em down will be da day aaaaaaall Hell breaks loose–foreva!"

That reminds me of everything my momma, the pastor and my granny used to say to me. They said, "a hard head will always make a soft behind, and we don't need a new one–literally speaking, not yet." After listening to this, I was a bit scared to have a "sweet thang," even after coming of age to do so.

I'm twenty-four now. I see the world a bit differently and I still haven't found time too make one (behind\baby). I remember my momma saying, "honey, take yo time. Let em come to you. Then I'd get confused at folks, who were sayin stuff like, "seek and ye shall find...." Well, I sought after a lot of things and all that I found wasn't all that I was looking for; like the troubles with the "sweet thangz" that I so willingly and ignorantly tasted of–only to find myself throwing it all back up, wishing I had never sampled their forbidden fruits. No, I'm not just talking about their worlds of pleasure. It was everything that they had ever delivered my way. Today, I walk down these streets myself, aware, saying, "don't do anything physically that would hinder you spiritually, becoz when you are messed up spiritually, you are too messed up mentally." Still, I ask myself, "where is the meaning / metaphor of life as I walk through this troubled town."

B.L.U.E.S. - Black Language, Ultimately Expressed in Song

The Poetic Soul

Introduction

It is an insatiable thing for an artist to create, tirelessly and exhaustively, until he / she has created his / her finest work. In like manner, I continuously commit my love and heart to paper, until the finest of manifestations materialize. Everyday, I've awakened to witness the heart in me beating a rhythm–an unorthodox tune that says many things....In my heart of hearts, when I write, the beats of my ball-point pen never palpitate the same way twice. This is what it says...

Brown Sugar Don't Melt

She's da moon I sees.
She's ma summer breeze.
She was the very first luv
dat ma soul had eva felt.
Let me tell you about my woman–Brown Sugar don't melt.
Her existence is that of a Purple Reign.
Her love is da soul's fruit for which I have feigned.
She's da raisin in da sun, the Ultimate One–
the first softness dat ma daddy eva felt
as he sowed his seeds to create another we,
singing, "Lawd, Brown Sugar just don't melt."
She makes me bed,
bakes ma beans,
brakes ma bread
and season's ma greens.
Whenever I needed prayer,
in humility she always knelt.
If there's anyone, whom I can count on,
it's the black woman,
coz Brown Sugar just don't melt.

Black Woman: Revolution

The Black Woman is Revolution and the Revolution of Life
in God's eyesight after Adam. She evolves from a very hot-spirited
and spiritual land, full of it's eclectic and the essence thereof.
My heart , my mind and my soul and the way I carry myself is the
very reflection
of the womb that carried me nine months long–age to age.
And I'll have you to know that in the 60's, I was not "born into
the revolution" as many would believe, but rather I was "born of
revolution"
–round, brown, wif ma hair slicked down,
only for it to be raised as a fro–
bright as da sun and big as da moon's glo,
singing those freedom songs that said,
"give me ma dashiki and ma afro wig
and I'll chant BLACK POWER, BLACK POWER
as I do my Negroes jig,"
For the Black Woman is Revolution and the Revolution of Life
in God's eyesight after Adam.
In the night, she says, " come to me. Come be my king
and my everything. I am the way back home. I am Mother*–
purposely and most-preciously perfected and personified.
Yes, the Black Woman is Revolution and the Revolution of Life
in God's eyesight after Adam–left of Adam's Rib.

Magnolia

She walked in and the weather changed.
The clouds dissipated and were no more,
with the Hue of Hues, dressed in blue,
Glory unseen heretofore.
Then she smiled warm and saintly,
melting the glaciers of heavy gloom.
The fresh air of God's precious presence filled my nostrils
as she entered the room.
Glory pierced my existence, wonderfully infiltrating
the abyss of my awkward loneliness,
Glory unseen heretofore,
God-graced Glory and now I'm blessed!
Magnolia-sweet sugar vine,
Ethereal Confection so divine,
tasting your presence, I experience what it's like to be whole.
Magnolia-sweet sugar vine,
the heaven I long to know!
You take me back to a sweeter time
where righteous lilies did grow,
where the Daughters of Zion sprang up in love from Holy Ground
and Holiness became them...
What Sweet, Amazin Grace!
What Sweet Sound!

Wishful Thinking

You never know a soul until you explore the heart.
Until then, you'll never appreciate the Human Work of Art.
You'll never feel the bloodracing bliss
until you clinch that first French Kiss.

Until then, you'll never know
that love that could grow.

Busy From The Mind–A Scolding

"Open rebuke is better than secret love."
–Proverbs

Spoke of me busy from the mind
not humbly from the heart.
Spoke of me like we never engaged–
worlds far apart.
When you were young and unbecoming,
I was paying my dues in tears
and now we've seen each other after all this time,
tell me, whose appreciated through the years?

My tutelage gave you shape and form,
catapulted you before the masses
and now you avoid the admission of being seated
at my wearied feet, absorbing all from my classes.
Do you despise my wearied feet after walking
miles in my shoes?
Do you regret the intellectual rearing, with which
you were infused?

You said I showed you the way–
enlightened you to the Masters.
Yet you would have been that sheep,
still led astray had I not been your first pastor.
So now that you're full grown and of age,
I sit emotionally halted in arrears,
after having help birth you into the spotlight,
but tell me who has depreciated through the years?
Tis a poor, cold and empty soul
that's forgotten their bridge
and forsaken their Elder's back.
she shall come to no fruition.
she shall always lack.
Girl, tell me about the child you were,

weathering the storm to cross the bridge
and how my life's work made you the lady that you are—
even when you didn't feel like a woman.
Tis a soul full of holes
that have forgotten their bridges
and forsaken their elder's back.
She shall come to no fruition. She shall forever lack.
Now tell me, which bridge brought you over?
Which black back saved your behind?
How dare you speak of me, not humbly from your heart,
yet busy from the mind?

Romantica:

Eden II (The Genesis Of 7's Park)

There she lay in love,
heated in the sunrays
of his heart's passion,
rubbing, feverishly, the holy, bald crown.
In their natural habitat,
flung back to a serene state,
the world was theirs.

No one told them they were naked yet.

Their innocence was Heaven fresh;
just a woman pleasing her man
and a man being pleased.

No one told them they were naked yet.

No one told them they were naked yet.

No one told them they were naked yet.

Eden–a place of waterfalls and madrigals,
crystal chrysanthemums, celestial streams
that echoed the sound of Cherubim wings.

Be it muddy Mississippi or Lake Michigan,
when I kissed you, the waters parted and I became
enthralled,
engulfed and entranced
into the dance
of the dew from your lips.
My soul rolled a thousand thunders,
orchestrated divinely as it made my body move
like Heaven making music,
sweet music,
holy and sacred music.

Everywhere Was Eden

Everywhere was Eden;
the gentle seas,
a brand new breeze
and the trees
with the leaves
that neva grieve.

Finally, I knew you–
who finally knew me–
who flew away with me into the hazeled rays of the sky's eye.
Spiritually speaking, your hands are always encoupled with mine.
Our bodies are always intertwined
And now I have my rib–
the craving that I have craved
since the dandy days in my blue-colored crib.

Dawn's eagles flew into the haze as we watched a flaming discus
hurling itself upward, in a clam, gentle manner,
to heat the somewhat hollow universe.

You laid in my arms, captivated by the creativity couples
are caressed with and possess. It's almost hard to describe
the I felt while we lay in the green grass, gladly glowing
as we glued ourselves side by side.

God married us and now we are one.

Laying there that morning, I felt like a brand new man;
finely formed out of the dark damp dust beneath me.
Everywhere was Eden;
the gentle seas,
a brand new breeze
and the trees
with the leaves
that neva grieve.

Nell

Every time I leave your home, I am gladly engulfed with great
gallons of gladness,
wonderfully overflowing, fine, fair, free, and everywhere without
care.

Our silence rings,
sings things,
it brings forth
solemn symphonies that sweetly season our ship saying,
"make my matrimony majestique,
sweet, sexy southern eyes,
take me back down the way
to where dewdrops delightfully danced
in a Durham, North Carolina rain–
where the sunlight's eyes rise high to the skies
and shine on a Mississippi \ Nile.

Coast with me as I float, smoothly along the soft, foamy shoreline–
where I laid my body's burden-anchored deep within the river of
Jordan.
Then sail with me wonderfully in matrimony
one glad morning down a Mississippi \ Nile–
where the sunlight's eyes rise high to the skies
and shine on my soul with a sanctified, southern smile.

The Sea Too Is Africa

The sea too is Africa.
I say that because it is green.
We were brought over here by a menace of monsters–
men who were so mean.

It is an awful red,
for in it, my family's blood was shed.
Yes, the sea too is Africa.

Finally, it is black and brown,
for in it, my family drowned
and

THE SEA TOO IS AFRICA!

Oh Ole Preacha Man

Oh, preacha man, preacha man can't you see?
I'ze in need of help and I wonsta be free.
Dun tried everythang dat a man like me can.
Oh listen to my words ole preacha man.
Preacha, I dun tried da ways of the world.
Dun had my share of the prettiest girls.
Got babies in just about every town.
Huh huh, I must admit, preacha, I have been around.
But oh preacha man, preacha man can't you see?
Been runnin for a long time and I wonsta be free.
Dun tried my luck at shootin up daisies-n-smokin wicked weed
and shackin wif all kind of crazies,
but dis heaya aint no life for me.
Oh ole preacha can't you see?

All I wants in my life is just to be changed,
but without you preacha man, my life is all deranged.

All I wants in my life is just to be free.
Preacha man, please say a prayer for me?

Sho Nuff Wooped

One of the worst woopins in the world
happened in the summer time,
shortly after begging my brother for bubblegum
and stealing my mother's dime.
The day I got caught, Hell never felt so real!
The lashes of lightening were so deeply imbedded
within my skin til I felt like slab of baby back ribs
on the 4th of July or some meaty piece of chicken,
sweltering in the heat, with tattoos of fine lines,
at a family reunion in the heat of August.
They say, "hell hath no fury like a woman scorned,"
but no fury can be compared to the fiery furnace
I fell in the day my butt was worn.
My only way out was to mumble and pout.
Then I went to sleep. It was over with and for the moment,
momma's job is done. Another hard head had made a softer behind.

Now that I am grown, she says, " a hard head will always make a
soft behind.
Can't play wif em babies. Gosta makem mind.
Train upa child in da way dat dey muss go,
and if dey don't like it, chile, dey can hit da dowe.
Aint got no room heah fa no grown niggas.
Coz, if you don't givem what dey need now,
dey just might get grown and give you da trigga."

My Beloved,

Tonight, I sit under the soft lights of my cozy living room, on the softest couch in the world, up next to a marshmallow like pillow, thinking only of you. Things would be so much better, if you were here with me. I know that we've only known each other for such a short time, but you've planted a seed within my heart. When I stand in your presence, I feel as if though I am a plant, being watered by the shadows of your smile, nurtured with all those healthy, wholesome hugs that you give. I've never felt an embrace that was so warm and sincere! Then, when I've missed you on a day such as today, I lean toward the morning sun, which bares a significant resemblance of you, because the very thoughts of you are as the rays of the sun, which forever shines upon me, beaming into my heart and mind.

A.J. II

She gives me sunlight during my travailing tenure,
under her tutelage.
Then, like a righteous and ready rocket, full of smart fire,
she ignites me and sends me soaring beyond the solar systems
and stars men have yet to discover,
for this world and that which is to come
is mine to conquer!

The Meaning Of Eulogy Square

Introduction

It is here, within the Boundaries of these four walls, of the following pages, that we pause to reflect upon the childhood that we so gratefully cherish. Here, we pay homage to the heroes that both, made and influenced our hearts.... Having gone on or remained, their actions serve as an important element of our oral tradition. By their lives, we've learned strong wisdoms. Hence the subtitle, *Eulogy Square*, for we dedicate it, humbly, to the moments of laughter, the legends and the elders etc. Eulogy Square reflects an era when you were a child and you had a childhood. It was the 60's, the 70's and the 80's, the music–no matter what record label. It was that favorite television program that we all sat around looking at–that favorite radio station that everybody listened to on Saturdays, as we were folding fresh, hot clean clothes, being informed as a people via modern talking drums, getting ready for church, studying the Sunday school lesson, while our mothers, aunts and sisters began ironing our Sunday's Best and cooking Sunday dinner. This is, in part, what life was like;

On HolyRollers

You know, we used to laugh at those before us called the Holy
Rollers,
but only Heaven knows what they mowed down in the Spirit
and cultivated in Faith and prayer as they sacrificed themselves
nightly
as vessels in the Holyghost fire laced floors,
molding as they were being molded–
paving the way through a desert of despair for the Joshua
generation.
They–the prayer warriors are the real Farmers of Faith–
the True Planters of Prayer,
the Honey makers of pure Holiness and
the Sewers of Sanctification.
Yes, they shall be the Reapers of Righteousness...
They shall never grow old.

Wednesdays

In my childhood, I spent a considerable amount of time at my grandmother's house (E.G.). Everyday before sunrise, she'd get up praying and moaning in one of those old Mississippi tones as she listened to her radio thereafter. The aroma of her favorite coffee ascended onto the second floor where we slept. Sometimes, I'd be the first one to sneak down stairs. We'd play hide and seek for a second. Then I'd emerge from beneath her kitchen table, asking for coffee. Her swift response shook me up suddenly saying, "boy, coffee a make you black!" That scared me and made me laugh simultaneously. I kinda believed it. Besides, who didn't believe their grandparent's every word, when they were a kid? She'd look out of her wooden, huntergreen screen door as the sunlight spilled through it and yell at all of the neighbors. All of her friends did it–they were sacred southern belles, ringing Sunday morning in everyday. They'd carry on conversations 500 feet away, four women at a time, sometimes without even yelling. You could hear every word plainly.

When they spoke, you knew what time it was. Stepfathers, fathers and sugar daddies, alike, would start up their car engines and be off to work. Clothes lines went up and fabric softener filled the air along with the smell of coffee, thick slab bacon and all kinds of breakfast food.

In the midst of the conversing, there was a man by the name of Daddy Price, whose window never stayed shut. He would always get the best of their conversation by buttin in and cracking a joke that had all of those women rolling with laughter. When my grandmother asked Daddy Price, how he was doing, he'd say rhythmically, "gotta get ova da hump baaabe!" By that time, lil ole Mrs. Price would just blush from beneath as she tended to her vegetable garden, picking out cabbage for the night's meal.

The other women looked at her so as to question, "girl, how did you put up with him all of these years?" Every time we saw Daddy Price or any of my grandmother's friends, we had to speak, no matter how many times we passed by them. It taught you something valuable. And when we'd see Daddy Price, and say hello, he'd say, "gotta get ova da hump baaabe! We'd love to mock him, playfully and wave just to hear him say it. Sometimes, he'd surprise us by stopping to ask us how we were doing! No matter what you told him, No matter how you felt or what you were going through, he responded with his now famous exclamation, "you gotta get ova the hump baaabe!"

Twenty plus years later–Daddy, Grandmone and some of her friends are now gone–The Southern Belles don't ring there anymore. The strong aromas of southern soul have dissipated. The gardens of greens and cabbage, with tall stalks of sweet corn looming above, have all faded.

Their homes have been renovated and converted into hundred-thousand dollar condos. I'm not hatin.

Yet, the words, the melodies, and the memories live on and at every impasse in life, it is there... that I hear good ole Daddy Price's words, out of the Windows of Memory saying, "you gotta get ova hump baaabe!"

Dessert: A Eulogy

(for my Daddy and family)

I have another grandmother by the name of Mary Jane Townsel (Weaver) and I love her dearly. To me, she's regal, majestic, myth and mystery as my mind's eye saw her. She reminds me, by her life, of Jesus Christ. You wonder how?

In January of 1996–the winter of her days, this side of Glory, she prepared me well for what was to come. In this conversation, I told her everything a lil boy always wanted to tell his grandma. She had her business fixed. She was ready to go Home. Six months later and half way into the new year, she ascended to Glory on High. Upon hearing this, I recounted every word of our very last conversation in January. And so my tears were...well, I just could not cry them. That would happen two years later.

As my uncle told me, on her last day, she was in the kitchen baking pies. The aroma of these pies filled the air–so much in so til the smell of them reached Heaven. After she had finished her pies, she turned off the stove. The pies were cooling and she sat down from her labors, to rest at the kitchen table. There she sat with her head propped up by her hand. The meal was complete. Dinner had been served and the Matriarch, Mary Jane went home. Yet, she did not go home without preparing dessert! When they found her, she or that shell of a woman, which was her, was seated upright at the table. Funny thing–the pies were still warm! Whatever became of them, I thought I dare not ask. As my uncle told it, "God smelled those pies and He wanted one for Himself!" And so, the cook went into the Kitchen of kitchens.

So, when you and I get to Glory Everlasting and feast, know that God is Almighty, Jesus Christ is the King of kings & Lord of lords, David the chief musician and the chief chef just might well be Mary Jane...and oh, we can't forget Aunt Eular with the handmade ice cream.

My Uncle Funny

Witty like Smitty,
Cool and laid back in comfort,
Savvy with a sophisticated greatness from the 60's,
The Fisherman Elite & Master Card Player,

A sexy bald man–that's why my aunt loved him so.
A sexy bald man–that's why my aunt loved him so.
A sexy bald man–that's why my aunt loved him so.

The man had a way with his words–nice and very smooth.
Baseball, hot-dogs and my aunt's cookin was his idea
of Saturdays, chillin in style with his favorite beer.
You knew when he came back with fish.
It would sho nuff be the night's dinner.
I think he was one of the realest of uncles that you could find.

You wore your hair in a way that made you an icon.
The Pure, Bold embodiment of a Black Man–
totally uncompromising Manhood. It's something
that you the other uncles and brothers at that time had.

You took care of house and home, freely as a man,
without question to your manhood.
You looked out for Sistah's mother, who had no man
of her own to do so.
You rained Hell, Fire and Brimstone on your boys in lecture.
You handled your girls with a fine grace, humorous with your
nieces and nephews–(always keep the one running joke–always).
Most of all, you kept that irresistible touch in your hands
that kept That Woman of Yours... Yours–
something so alive. I see I got it from my Daddy.
And he from his... so on and so forth etc.

Long live the Card Maverick
at every table, where deuces be wild.
Long live Uncle Funny,
The Sweet, Bald Summer's Child!

Brown Bard Of The Baptist Church

A man of degrees,
whose well traveled road stretch back far!
How far does he sees!

Master Orator, teller of The Story is he.
The Walking Proverb, wrapped full of allegory–
a testimony for you and I.

Oh, what would I to be!
Aside: As The Blueprint designed.

Every place in life I traveled, he taught,
would either shape and build me
or erode and utterly destroy me.

"Son, watch where you carry yourself
and the basket which you prepare as gift.
Either the sweet fruit would turn sour
or it would make the best of pies,
with a scent so strong til it gets God's eyes.
Either let it rot or it'll make the best preserves
to bestow upon that one woman,
whom you deem deserves."

He was in our eyes
a philosopher and great thinker,
a well of wisdom–
a concierge of the craft,
who invited us saying,
"come be a drinker of Wisdom
and absorb what ye will.
Come. Be and consume with your mind
and take your fill.

The Church will have their speakers, preachers
and deacons that pray loud, long and hard,
but only at the Sunrise, this side of Glory,
will you find the BROWN BAPTIST BARD!

49

The Silhouettes of Soul

The excellence of every art
must consist in the complete
accomplishment of its purpose.
–Anonymous

(Found inscripted on a historic building in Printer's Row in
Chicago)

Natural High–1990

Five years ago
from the valley low,
I could not sink or swim.
The wall built by me called "Round"
was now torn down.
The love within was sound,
yet the one for whom I longed
could not be found.
Then eyes were laid on you and my feet hit the ground.
Five years later, Berlin's my almamater.
No experience could have ever been greater!
I shall take flight to the sky.
That's where you will find me–
on a natural high in 1990.

The Secrets I Kept

I looked into a mirror.
No beauty I saw.
An undeveloped fellow
like talent that's raw,
so full of life and energy–
full of love, hopes and dreams,
like a hot spring bursting upward
til it forms ever-peaceful streams.
Then came you;
the Molder, the Great Heartshaper,
the Love, the Rose, the Great Heartbreaker.
You loved me and left.
I mourned and wept,
but the secrets of the love you gave...I kept.

Black Romanticism

If dreams and wishes were horses,
I'd fain to be your stallion.
If I were all the jewelry you'd look upon,
my only hope would be to be worn
about the neck as your medallion.
If you were the heavens and I was the earth,
my only wish would be to sit beneath you golden hearth–
to feel your goodness–
to feel your charm
and to be near a heart that is oh so warm.
If your love was my well,
it would never run dry,
for true love lives forever,
by and by!

Feel–So–Sorry Syndrome

Tomorrow is another day
and a new one at that.
Tomorrow just may be
another Mt. Top experience.
Will I go up? Will I dive
with the next landslide
that comes along?
ASIDE: "ONLY BE STRONG!"
I left my baby somewhere in the past.
Somethings' just aren't meant to last.
When morning came,
I felt no good fortune or fame.
Now the love is lost
and the excuse is lame.

Love In Her Queensize Bed

Another month has passed.
Love has come and gone.
Another love has left her name to carry on.
A winter's love have I loved that I now dread.
A winter's love that we made warm
in her queensize bed.
Today is a new day.
Her love is passed away, but what's ironic about it all,
I'm not full of dismay.
These were the days that I loved without a heart.
That's what made leaving her easy
when it was time to part.
A winter's love have I loved that I now dread.
A winter's love that we made warm in her queensize bed.

The Open Letter:
A Talking Drum Speaks

It is cited as culturally criminal: the crying shame
And understood in the utmost of terms why such ostracizing
Has taken place. And behold, the mask is fallen from your face.
You have sold the birthright of the Black Aesthetic for the porridge of
penniless pennies and worthless, withered greens. And so the generation behind you. they may not be heard
All because, to them, you were not true. You could not keep your word.
Your rhythm has ceased and its heart's beat has flatlined into false-
hoods, as you lay comatose–commercialized in heresies that laud only
you. You have not paved the way. Rather you've broken up the road and
those behind you bare the bloody trek with blisters, in bitterness. You've
relinquished the rhythm makers and thus, we renounce you. You have
not planted nor watered. What shall become of thee, oh fig tree? Why
have you not brought forth any fruit? Would the righteousness of those
lilies spinning beneath you, out shine you as they spiraled upward? Is
the sky so low that these behind you should not grow? The Ants of
Annihilation, in your mind, consume you else they would have been
brain cells used to cultivate and catapult the crop of colors into the universe. Your Chloe is only the kiss of death, division, denial and rejec-
tion. Faulty Renegade, thou hast ravished thine own garden, plundered
and pillaged the precious pearls, pouncing upon their hearts and grind-
ing them into a powerless powder. Caution–ignite them and they are
prepared to blow in your face and reluctantly infiltrate and invigorate
your nostrils with a smoke that makes one envious.

Your lack of inclusion has given us disillusions. Your movement, while
philosophically and intellectually stimulating, has caused a falling
away and the segregating.

And now we, left to ourselves, define ourselves, not even by the thing
that made you–you. But rather by the righteous rhythm makers and
their vibes that yet remain true.

Once upon a time, all one had was their word and their good name. These days, they'll try to steal your words and kill them. And what's to become of the good name? It is assassinated before it ascends and you –the rhythmless killer–ridiculous and vicious vibe snatcher hath abounded all the more with stolen goods and accolades. Meanwhile, you rebuttal the lifeless victim by saying, "it's only business." NO! The business of the Black Aesthetic and blaculturvation, more precious than gold, was to be true in word, keeping the flame lit, thus being true to thine ownself and those to come. What say you to the talking Drum?

The Summer Sonnet of 1991

You showed me love.
You loved me again.
Oh precious friend,
please, take my hand.
Baby, walk with me
when you can.
Stand by my side.
I'll be your man.
I'll give you all of me
like you deserve.
Let my hands be the balm that calms your nerves.
I'll eva love you and take that stand.
Just stand by my side.
I'll be your man.

C–Note: She Moves Me

Scientifically, she came to me, aglowing bright as high noon.
She soared past as a comet and a shooting star.
But what stopped her in all of her virtuous, majestical velocity
was the mighty magnetism Heaven embedded within my soul

And she moved me...Yes, she moved me.

What stopped her soaring was that her meteor shower
melted my senses–my immune system's defenses
and I became We...as she found her way
through my black hole of awkward loneliness - bound
to be my Bride,
to be my Blessing,
my Bone of Honey...of Sweetness.

I was limbless.
I was lifeless,
but her cataclism and its chloe
made me whole!

Her perfume, glistening as the milky way,
infiltrated my stratosphere & atmosphere.
Ever so near is she that I breathe her existence.
I am on fire, riding high with her and together,
we never past the same way for centuries as

She moves me.....Oh, how she moves me.

Musically, she is the melodious of movements,
flowing fervently out of the loins and horns of Africa,
catching me and sweeping me til I swirl, spinning down
into her whirlpool, descending into the decadence of her depths.
And when I am lifeless, she lifts me up to breathe...her.
Symbolic of Mother Earth, if she quakes, I am unbalanced
and if she yields her fruit, then I am in tune...
more than all the jazz of June,

For she moves me...Yes, she moves me!

She Moved Me & God Made Her Mine!

Acknowledgments

The Bible tells me to acknowledge God in all of my ways and He will direct my paths. To that end, I give Him the glory for the things He has done. I thank Him for His everlasting creativity–a special speck of which he embedded in this dusty, complex frame of mine. He gave it to me so that I may cast it upon the waters of the world in love, sowing it as talent and not burying it low. If there be any glory, honor and praise, Father, it's yours. I'd like to acknowledge my Pastor, The Honorable Prophetess Dr. Hattie B. Jones–a very strong influence in my life.

Good shadows of great things to come came in an array of light, with a cast of thousands in upper Academia. The place is Columbia College. The year was 1990. My college professors, peers and mentors, alike, gave birth to the monumental moments and memories that I'll treasure forever. Thank you ANGELA JACKSON, first and foremost for your tutelage, your love, your patience, wit, wisdom and understanding. I thank you for the rebuke, correction and nipping bad things in the bud early. It's because of you that a young man like me wouldn't die, at heart, and didn't retreat, down in Florida, back in '92 at N. A. S. D. A. (National Association of Speech & Dramatic Arts).

Neither did I leave Florida A & M empty-handed and dissatisfied. Between every line, you're that foundation-that root upon which I stand, rest and grow. Yes, I am proud to be the fruit of your literary vine and your fruit in progress. Working with you is humbling, because I never know what's going to erupt from your creative soul.

Just before the Columbia Experience, my friend, Wendy Barriteau-Johnson, encouraged me to make this project happen. This is the first, humble realization of that encouragement. My expression(s) herein, contained, are not written because I just felt like I had something to say. My sincere desire is to add to that cultural fabric of literature at large. By doing so, I aim to illuminate the heavy laden heart from the dross and drudgery of life. I believe that my purpose in writing is to create responsibly and respectfully. Prayerfully.

About The Author

Marcel Townsel is a Chicago native and a graduate of Columbia College Chicago. He is an active participant in the affairs of his church and resides in Chicago with his family.

To purchase a copy of this book, send a money order / check to:
BTSR @
Townsel Communications Co.
P.O. Box 0542
Chicago, IL 60690-0542

A portion of the proceeds will be donated to charity.

All returned (NSF) checks will be assessed $20.00.